Reader Reviews on the Juggernaut App

'An excellent read, and not only for people with a broken heart. Very well written and structured. A treat to read. Looking forward for more books of Dr Shyam Bhat' —**Sabina Basha**

'Really nice book'—**Vidhyaniwas**

'Not only for the ones who are going through breakups, but should also be read by the ones who are single and prone to feeling lonely. This book helped me to value myself more. I keep re-reading the book in parts whenever I need some affirmation'—**Ananya Ghosh**

'I'm not one for self-help kind of books in general, but this book makes so much sense as it helps you understand the scientificity of your feelings. And... it's just the right length too!'—**Sneha L**

'I went through the book in less than days. I started with my quest for answers to heartbreak and its causes and consequences. I had some memories I wanted to examine in the light of knowledge I was reading. I ended up by learning many things and in fact unlearning many as well. The author has deconstructed and demystified many things. I think I will handle myself better not from the point of view of a heart, but from the viewpoint of human rationality. The respect for eastern science may grow now onwards inside me. A must read for all. Don't miss this man and woman'—**Jitendra**

'Awesome'—**Kosana**

'Lucidly written. Very easy to comprehend even for a lay person. Most important, it is not only useful for heartbroken people but also to those who suffer from dysfunction of any other intimate relationship. The book gave me gave me deep insights into human emotions. Thank you'—**Kanti Khanvte Hodarkar**

'Clear and without fluff. Love the pointedness of the solution provided. 9/10 would recommend'—**Tanzila Anis**

'Though the book is short, it provided some much needed ointment to heal a broken heart. The author writes as if he's speaking to the reader and the reader, thus, forms a connect instantly. Very, very cogent arguments, and true understating of human relationships in the Indian context make this book a worthwhile read'—**Rahul Sharma**

'This book is like the Bhagwad Geeta for heartbreaks. Every time you read it, the book throws up different aspects, clearer thoughts. It is therapeutic'—**Anklesh Agarwal**

'Good book'—**Tummalapalli**

'A great read! To the point and very concisely written... Eases the mind...'—**Gayatri Behera**

'Great book to get over a heartbreak'—**Lakshaya Sachdeva**

'I read this book in one sitting. We need more information on this subject. And we need credible writing as well. Thank you. It's a good book'—**Ganesh Pol**

You Will Love Again

A Guide to Healing from Heartbreak

Dr Shyam Bhat

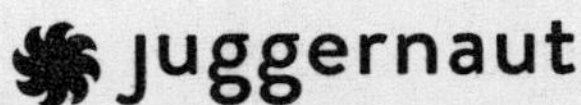

JUGGERNAUT BOOKS
KS House, 118 Shahpur Jat, New Delhi 110049, India

First published by Juggernaut Books 2016

The client stories in this book are composites of real cases; however, names and details have been changed to protect the clients' identities.

ISBN 9788193237281

Typeset in Adobe Caslon Pro by R. Ajith Kumar, New Delhi

Printed at Manipal Technologies Ltd

To the women who broke my heart – you taught me what books can't teach about love and loss.

To the many people, men and women, who share their stories of heartbreak with me – you inspire me with your courage, resilience and strength. It's a privilege to facilitate your journey to healing.

Contents

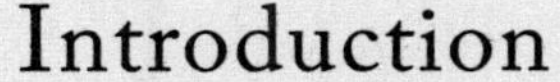

Introduction

So she left you. Or he doesn't return your calls any more. Your love has ended. Your heart is broken. And you are reading this wondering – what is this guy going to tell me that my friends don't tell me? What does he have to offer that the Internet and countless agony aunt columns have not taught me?

Here's what's different about this book. First, it is born of experience. I too have ended relationships and suffered. But then, so has most of the world. The difference is that I am also a psychiatrist. And as a psychiatrist, I have seen heartbreak in countless people who have come to me suffering from feelings of sadness and pain, and I experienced these same emotions in myself, and wondered – what is the strange nature of this experience that even the most rational mind cannot seem to change?

The pain of heartbreak is mysterious. It comes from the deepest reaches of our being, our mind, our body and our soul, and when we learn to deal with heartbreak, both to heal and then to love again, we discover the best part of us.

As a psychiatrist, I have learned to take this emotional experience seriously, for it is at the root of a great many emotional disturbances. I have seen people whose lives, after the end of a relationship, have spiralled out of control, degenerating into addictions, meaningless relationships and illnesses, battling loneliness and problems in their careers and, in the worst instances, ending in suicide.

In fact, the leading cause of suicide among the youth appears to be heartbreak-related depression. **More than 1.35 lakh people commit suicide in India every year and as many as 20,000 of them end their life because of heartbreak.**

For many of us, heartbreak is our first really

deep emotional experience. This means that it can shape us and our relations with others forever. You fall in love with her and you feel like you have never felt before. You are obsessed with her and then one day she leaves you for someone else. Or perhaps you started out as friends and before you knew it he became the one person you could pour your heart out to.

The one person who understood you completely, the one person who accepted you completely in a way that no one else did before. And then one day he leaves for another town and breaks up with you. Now you see his profile on Facebook, you see his pictures, you see him with someone else – and you cannot understand how you can ever be happy again.

Whatever your situation, this book can help you not just to get over heartbreak but also to benefit from the experience. A great suffering such as heartbreak is an opportunity for you to learn to look within, and to discover your own greatness, strength, peace and happiness.

This book, I hope, will give you insights that can help you become happier, stronger and more complete and in the future help you to love again and have a better relationship.

How to Use This Book

This book is short but it is packed with information. It first looks at what happens to your body and your mind (chapter 2) when you suffer from this trauma. Then it asks the most important question of all, why does it hurt so much (chapter 3) and finally I take you on the path to healing (chapters 4 and 5). At the end of the book, in the appendix, I have also given advice on diet, meditation and exercise and put in an FAQ which addresses the most common questions I get asked.

Through the book I have included exercises that are designed to help you heal and grow from the experience of heartbreak. Take your time to read and reflect, and to answer the questions completely.

Take This Questionnaire to Find Out How Much Heartbreak Has Hurt You

Consider each of these statements, and mark how strongly you agree or disagree with these statements (compare how you feel currently with how you used to feel before the break-up). Answer the questions honestly and without thinking too much about it.

Strongly disagree:	**0**
Disagree:	**1**
Neither agree nor disagree:	**2**
Agree:	**3**
Strongly agree:	**4**

1. I am angrier than I used to be
2. I feel more tired than usual
3. Life does not seem interesting any more
4. Life is boring
5. I feel lonely
6. I feel bad about how I look
7. I feel bad about who I am

8. I cannot stop thinking about my loved one
9. I find myself having thoughts about violence against her/him
10. I want to die
11. I don't see any reason to live
12. I can't sleep well
13. I don't feel like eating
14. I don't feel like meeting anyone
15. I believe that love is for fools
16. I regret falling in love with her/him
17. I hope we will get back together if I wait long enough
18. I am sad
19. I don't think I can love again
20. I have lost/gained a lot of weight
21. I believe that nobody else will love me like she/he did
22. I believe that nobody else will understand me the way he/she did
23. I am incomplete without her/him
24. I miss how she/he looks/smells/feels

Your Heartbreak Meter

Score

75 to 96: Severe heartbreak

50 to 75: Significant heartbreak

25 to 50: Moderate heartbreak

8 to 25: Minimal heartbreak

If you have any thoughts of suicide, you are suffering from severe heartbreak, even if there are no other symptoms. Do not do anything to hurt yourself. Seek professional help asap. Call a suicide helpline now. Please do not wait or hesitate. For a list of therapists in your area, please see http://thelivelovelaughfoundation.org. *Remember, you will feel love again.*

1

What's Happening to Your Body and Mind?

Your Body

'I can't sleep at night, I lie awake thinking of him, I don't want to eat, I don't want to meet anyone. Life is so grey and empty without him. My body is in pain. My heart literally aches for him.'

'When she broke up with me, I felt as if someone had kicked me in the stomach. I was angry. I hated all women, I think I hated everyone. I was drinking every night, at least half a bottle of whisky, smoking more than two packs a day. Looking back, I was in so much pain, I wanted to die.'

Heartbreak is an emotionally devastating experience, and most people who experience it have never felt such pain before. People often describe their feelings to me as if they were feeling sensations in their body. The pain is real, they tell me. And they are right.

No Difference Between Physical and Romantic Pain

The same part of the brain that is activated in physical pain is activated when you are suffering from heartbreak. In other words, as far as your brain is concerned, the end of romantic love is equivalent to your body being traumatized, as if a part of it has been brutally amputated.

It's Like Having Withdrawal Symptoms

The part of the brain – the caudate nucleus – that is connected to drug addiction is activated in heartbreak, causing obsession and craving. You feel bad just like the heroin addict who has not got the drug, and I am not speaking metaphorically.

Research shows that the pain of heartbreak decreases when people are given morphine (I am not telling you to take morphine or any such drug; in fact, the risk of drug addiction during heartbreak is high since the body is craving release from the pain).

Dr Helen Fisher, a psychologist who conducted path-breaking research in heartbreak, studied the brains of people who had been recently rejected by their partner but were still in love. Dr Fisher scanned these people's brains while they looked at the photograph of their loved one and then again as they looked at a photo of an acquaintance and compared the respective brain activity.

The results were shocking: heartbreak seemed to cause the same brain changes seen in a drug addict who is withdrawing from powerful drugs such as cocaine. Both cocaine and being in love cause the release of a chemical called dopamine and stimulate a part of the brain called the mesolimbic system, the reward centre of the brain, causing an intense feeling of pleasure, ecstasy and euphoria.

When love (or the drug) is taken away, the mesolimbic dopaminergic system of the brain slows down – the person comes crashing down from the high of love (or the drug), the brain starts to crave the jolt of dopamine and this is felt as intense pain, withdrawal and craving. Normal life in contrast now seems dull and colourless, and the cocaine addict and the heartbroken person will now intensely crave and seek the source of reward and pleasure.

Your Hormones Are Affected Too

Other studies showed that heartbreak also depletes chemicals in the brain called endorphins – these chemicals are natural painkillers and the depletion of endorphins causes real physical and emotional pain.

Heartbreak increases levels of the hormone called cortisol, which is secreted by the adrenal glands. This can cause weight gain, fatigue, body aches and pains and a weakened immune system, which can make you more susceptible to cold and infections.

Heartbreak Can Literally Break Your Heart

Although very rare, a condition called takotsubo cardiomyopathy can occur during times of extreme emotional stress such as heartbreak: when the mind and emotional heart are threatened and hurt, the body releases huge amounts of stress hormones such as adrenaline, which in large doses are toxic to the heart. In severe cases, these chemicals weaken and damage the heart muscle – the walls of the heart become thin and the heart swells like a balloon, unable to pump blood adequately, causing shortness of breath, chest pain and, on rare occasions, death.

Your Mind

The researcher and doctor Elisabeth Kübler-Ross studied the emotional reactions of people who had lost a loved one to an illness, and this research was later extended to people undergoing heartbreak. According to this research, when you undergo heartbreak, you will experience the following emotions:

- **Denial**
- **Anger**
- **Bargaining**
- **Depression**
- **Acceptance**

These emotions are not necessarily experienced in this order, and a person undergoing heartbreak will often feel a roller coaster of emotions, passing from one stage to another or sometimes experiencing all at the same time. To this range of emotions, I would like to add a few more: fear, guilt, regret and shame. If you suppress these feelings, you can experience a lingering numbness.

Fear

'I woke up in the middle of the night and my heart was beating so fast I thought I was getting a heart attack. I couldn't breathe, I couldn't think, I was so scared, and I didn't know what I was really scared of.'

'I don't know if I will every meet anyone again. I am so afraid that I will be alone forever. I can't focus at work because I am thinking of her all the time. I am so tense and have become so impatient that I shout for small things and then I feel bad.'

Your brain, like that of all animal species, is designed to protect you, and it does this by alerting you to any potential threat. Fear is a signal that comes from the almond-shaped amygdala – this fear centre of the brain signals threat even before the conscious brain can process the reasons for the fear.

The loss of a significant relationship is a threat to your emotional self and to your identity, and so the amygdala becomes hyperactive during heartbreak, signalling excessive threat and fear.

The body also releases stress hormones such as adrenaline and norepinephrine. These chemical changes trigger the fight, flight or freeze mode. Your muscles become tight, your breath becomes rapid, your stomach clenches, your heart rate increases. Emotionally you may feel scared or anxious, nervous or hyperactive. You may feel more irritable and angrier than usual. Your appetite decreases or you may experience cravings for unhealthy food. If stress persists – and it often does with heartbreak – then hormones such as cortisol are elevated, causing a cascade of physical problems such as fatigue, impaired immunity and impairment of brain function, including worsening memory and elevated risk of depression.

Events that evoke intense emotions are emblazoned in the brain – this is true for positive as well as negative emotions.

You never forget the first time you fell in love. You never forget the first time your heart was broken.

Your mind, now under threat, will start to see more

negatives than positives, seeing danger when none exists or feeling more insecure in other areas of your life. Your self-esteem may take a beating, as your body and mind experience sadness, anxiety and turmoil and as you lose the source of self-affirmation.

But why does the brain feel threat? After all, the end of a relationship is not an attack on your physical self. So why then does the brain react in this manner?

The brain cannot differentiate between the physical self and the psychological self, or identity. When you lose an important relationship, psychologically speaking, you lose a part of yourself. This threat to the emotional self is perceived as a threat to the physical self and the brain reacts to heartbreak as if your very life was threatened.

Fear is normal – the only people who do not feel fear are those with a serious brain disorder. The problem is that in modern living, these ancient, powerful, primal protective mechanisms are often inappropriately activated: the subtle threats of modern life cause omnipresent anxiety, inhibiting countless people, holding them back from pursuing their dreams.

In heartbreak these same brain mechanisms go into overdrive. The loss of a loved one is one of the biggest emotional threats you can face and your brain will respond to this with great fear.

Anger

'Holding on to anger is like grasping a hot coal with the intent of throwing it at someone else; you are the one who gets burned.'—The Buddha

Although anger is more common in men, women too suffer from anger. The anger could be one (or more) of four types:

1. Anger directed at the ex
2. Anger directed at yourself
3. Anger directed at the world: anger towards the world, towards women, towards love

4. Subtle anger that becomes cynicism or sadness

Mahesh became bitter after his fiancée broke up with him a few months before the wedding. 'I'll never ever open myself to anyone like I did with her. I'll make sure I'm never used again. Nobody's worth it.' He started smoking more; he stopped eating right, sleeping well and bothering about his looks. When we met his breathing was irregular, his hands clenched (he seemed almost ready to attack). He was a cornered animal, reacting against a rejecting world.

Anger is easier to deal with when it is obvious. But after heartbreak, anger can become deep and subtle, expressed as a mixture of cynicism and hostility towards the world. Research also shows that heart attacks are much more likely in people suffering from what's called 'cynical hostility'.

When Sushma's heart was broken, she too felt angry. But her anger was expressed as a general irritability. She snapped at her parents and friends, and became more impatient at work. Her body too ached and she was tired all the time, but was not sure why. When she thought about how her boyfriend had wronged her, her stomach contracted with pain.

Many people undergoing heartbreak desire revenge and retribution and, in the worst cases, people even physically hurt the person who has broken their heart. Some try to get even by venting on Facebook or posting 'revenge pictures' of their ex in compromising positions.

Men and women both experience anger, though they often express it in different ways.

Men are more prone to acts of violence, sometimes even hurting their ex because anger has clouded their thinking and rationality – there are many unfortunate instances of ex boyfriends who have assaulted and even murdered their exes. Others don't vent their anger; instead the anger simmers along and permeates their being until it seems to take up permanent residence, changing their personality and outlook to life.

To know if you are angry about the break-up, answer these questions honestly:

- Do I fantasize or think about 'getting even' with my ex?
- Do I feel that I have been hurt by my ex and do I hunger for retribution and revenge?
- Do I have a difficult time sleeping?
- Do I have tension in my jaw, neck, chest or abdomen?
- Do I have more road rage than usual?
- Have I become more impatient?
- Do I find myself thinking cynical thoughts such as 'the world is a cruel place', 'I hate people', 'I hate women', 'men cannot be trusted', or 'love is for losers'?

Healing from Anger

The most important step in healing from anger is to understand it. Understand that your anger comes from hurt. Instead of feeling sadness, some of your hurt has become anger. Releasing this anger is good and holding it in is bad, especially for your health in the long term. But you have to release and express this anger in a safe way, in a way that won't cause you permanent harm. Indeed, you should try to understand what this anger is teaching you.

To get over anger, first answer the following questions:

- Do you find yourself thinking angrily about the end of your relationship?
- Do you find yourself angry with your ex and thinking about revenge and retribution?
- Is your body manifesting any signs of repressed or suppressed anger such as elevated blood pressure, increased heart rate, muscle tension, physical restlessness, shallow or rapid breathing?

Exercise

- Write down all the events that made you angry. Putting down your angry and painful thoughts will help release some painful memories. It will also give the rational part of your brain a chance to examine these thoughts.

- Write down all the times that you may have caused the other person some pain. We sometimes forget that we too cause pain to those who are close to us. Acknowledging the hurt that you've caused will help you feel less victimized. Maybe the pain came from the relationship rather than from the other?

Denial

'It's just a phase. He/she will eventually see the light and come back to me.'

'I don't believe him when he tells me he doesn't love me any more. I know he still loves me deep down.'

A common reaction when we are faced with profound loss is to deny that it is happening. I have worked with countless people who refuse to accept that their relationship is over.

Driven by denial, you may continue to communicate with your ex, sending him or her messages, unable to get on with your life. Many people even stay single, keeping themselves available, hoping that their ex will come back into their lives.

To deny what is clear to everyone else is actually a psychologically draining and exhausting task. The subconscious mind has to ignore all evidence that the relationship is over and instead seek hope where there is little. Denial ultimately causes further pain and distress and prolongs the misery of heartbreak.

Bargaining

'God, please give her/him back to me. I will stop eating non-veg, and give up anything, if only you get her back to me.'

'Please come back to me, I will change, I will

give you anything you desire, just come back to me.'

'I am begging you, please give me one more chance.'

So many men and women, strong and self-reliant, independent and autonomous, are devastated by heartbreak, reduced to begging and pleading with their partners to come back. Bargaining is your mind's way of shielding you from the terror you feel when you consider the end of your relationship. Unfortunately, as a coping mechanism, bargaining diminishes your self-esteem, making you even more fragile and dependent.

Bargaining may also prompt you to make promises you cannot keep or behave in ways that are contradictory to your own true nature. If you find yourself bargaining, begging and pleading, know that this is also a symptom of heartbreak. When you begin to work on and improve your self-esteem, you will finally be able to let go.

Depression

Any significant emotional stress can lead to depression, and heartbreak is one of the most stressful situations of them all.

About 40 per cent Indians carry a variant of the serotonin transporter gene, which makes them vulnerable to depression. ***This means that 40 per cent of our country could suffer from depression if they experience significant emotional stress such as heartbreak.***

Depression is not the same as sadness, although it may feel similar. Major depressive disorder, which is the full medical name for the disorder commonly called depression, is a condition where brain function itself is altered as a result of stress.

Most people find it difficult to understand depression. It seems like sadness and since we have all experienced sadness, you may think that you can snap out of the lows of depression too.

But depression is more than just sadness. As the brain alters in its function due to stress, a person suffering from major depressive disorder will feel a sadness and mood that is unlike anything they may have experienced before.

The writer William Styron, who wrote about it in his memoir *Darkness Visible*, eloquently describes the pain: 'My brain had begun to endure its familiar siege: panic and dislocation, and a sense that my thought processes were being engulfed by a toxic and unnameable tide that obliterated any enjoyable response to the living world.'

A person suffering from depression can feel as if his brain has slowed down or stopped, as if a dark veil separates him from the world. He feels low, sad or irritable. Life seems oppressive and nothing is enjoyable.

It is important to understand that this lack of positivity is not due to a bad attitude and cannot be changed by positive thinking alone (as pop psychologists might suggest).

Depressed people may experience any or all of the following: sadness, nervousness, lethargy, fatigue, irritability, changes in sleep pattern and appetite (either too little or too much), guilt, lower self-esteem, body ache and poor concentration and memory. In severe cases, people may feel hopeless and worthless, which may lead them to contemplate suicide.

If you feel you may have depression, click the link below to assess your symptoms

http://healthnet.umassmed.edu/mhealth/ZungSelfRatedDepressionScale.pdf

If you suspect you have major depressive disorder, do not hesitate to contact a psychologist or psychiatrist.

Regret

Two emotions tie you to the past – regret and guilt. Regret is the feeling that you could have averted a bad outcome by doing something differently. Regret is the feeling that says 'if only', 'I shouldn't have done this' or 'I should have done that'.

We can feel regret because the human brain possesses the ability to think of multiple alternative futures. The parts of your brain called the prefrontal cortex and the orbitofrontal cortex can project yourself into the future, comparing and contrasting what is with what could have been.

Regret occurs when you compare your current state with 'what could have been' or, in other words, when you compare reality with fantasy.

Your brain makes you believe that the fantasy – which seems like the better version of reality – would have become reality if only you had acted differently. The greater the disparity between your current reality and the fantasy idealized reality, the worse your pain.

So, for example, Rita said, 'If only I had spoken to my parents about Amit, we would have been together.' She is currently married to someone she describes as a good man, but she cannot let go of what might have been with Amit.

'What would life have been like with Amit?' I asked.

'It would have been wonderful. We would have

travelled and had long and deep conversations. We were soulmates,' she replied.

'But you only met him two or three times, so maybe you don't know what it would have been like with him,' I said.

'I just know,' she said. 'And we would have been together if only I had not been such a coward.'

Rita's current state – that of being in a reasonably happy and stable relationship – is compromised by regret. She had met Amit only a few times – not enough time to assess compatibility for a long-term relationship, no matter how powerful the attraction or chemistry, and her mind and brain had taken the intensity and connection of those brief encounters and projected it into the future, creating the perfect fantasy.

No reality can compete with fantasy, and so Rita continued to struggle, unable to enjoy the present, the regret of heartbreak shackling her to the past.

The pain of regret comes from comparing your present with a fantasy. What you are regretting is a potential outcome, not a real event.

If you are suffering from regret after heartbreak, you are probably self-critical in other areas as well. Perfectionists often carry a lot of regret.

Please stop torturing yourself needlessly.

Guilt

Guilt is similar to regret, but subtly different. Regret says, 'I wish it hadn't been so.' Guilt says, 'I did a bad thing.'

As with most of these emotions, in order to get over guilt, we must listen to its teachings. ***We must answer the question 'What is guilt trying to tell me about myself?' Once we learn from guilt, we can gently let it go.***

Geeta cheated on her boyfriend and she couldn't stop thinking about it. When she told him, they broke up. She left the relationship feeling tormented and confused. 'Is he right? Am I a bad person?' When she was able to pause and reflect on why she had gone against her value system, she realized her guilt carried a powerful message: she was in a relationship that wasn't giving her what she needed. 'I know now that I'm not comfortable with infidelity and the next time this happens I will be better equipped to handle the real issue.' This experience of guilt and heartbreak helped her understand herself better.

Shame

'I can't help feeling love for him, even though he cheated on me. I know I should hate him, I know I should not want to see him ever again. But I am so weak that I think if he came back to me, I would go back, even though I know he will cheat on me again. I feel so bad, so ashamed of loving him.'

While guilt is a useful emotion, shame is not. Shame is a toxic, hurtful emotion and one that you must identify and let go of.

What is the difference between guilt and shame? They feel similar, in that both guilt and shame are the feeling of discomfort and emotional pain that you experience after you have done something that you deem 'bad' or contrary to your values.

However, shame is deeper than guilt. If you have done something that is bad, guilt is the emotion that says 'My behaviour was not good' while shame is the emotion that says 'I am not good.' Guilt is feeling bad about your behaviour and shame is feeling bad about who you are.

Heartbreak can evoke feelings of deep shame and if not managed properly this shame can be overwhelming and can lead to depression and hopelessness. Working through shame will help you become more aware of your true strengths, value and worth.

Numbness

Our body and mind are always trying to protect us from pain. Sometimes this causes further distress.

When you are going through heartbreak, you may, as many people do, try to suppress the pain.

Do not do that – because when our mind pushes away and blocks bad feelings, it suppresses good feelings too.

As far as our brain is concerned, there are no 'bad' and 'good' feelings – all feelings are important and to be acknowledged. If we do not, then feelings disappear, and we are left with an absence of feeling, a numbness that you may not be aware of. If you are not careful, the numbness can linger for months, even years, after the trauma.

I have worked with many people who, after a heartbreak, could not love again. Worse, they were unaware that they were numb, until a family member or a friend brought it to their notice.

Those who are numb from the trauma of heartbreak may get into other bad relationships since they do not know what really gives them happiness. Take the case of Niraj.

A few years after his divorce he met a pleasant girl. 'I am going to marry her,' he said, without much joy or pleasure. When I turned his attention to his emotions and feelings, he was surprised to realize that he had very little feeling. His heartbreak had resulted in so much pain that he was subconsciously afraid to feel again. Now he was making a decision based on logic and practicality. Emotional pain like heartbreak is prolonged and becomes complicated when the emotions are blocked and held within.

When you connect with feelings again, you may feel pain initially. But this pain will give way to a positive feeling. When you connect with feeling, then you are fully alive, to live and to love again.

2

Why Does It Hurt So Much?

What happens in heartbreak? Why does it hurt so much? Why does it feel like you are going to die, or that you would like to end it all? Why does everything around you seem so lifeless and colourless, and the future so empty? Why does everything remind you of your lover? Why do you obsess, unable to forget, tormented by thoughts of your loved one?

Attachment

'I'm never gonna dance again / The way I danced with you.'

—'Careless Whisper', George Michael

'I carry a smile when I'm broken in two / And I'm nobody without someone like you / I'm trembling inside / And nobody knows it but me.'
—'Nobody Knows', The Tony Rich Project

'The reason it hurts so much to separate is because our souls are connected.'
—*The Notebook*, Nicholas Sparks

When a serious relationship ends it is almost as if a part of you has died. Many books, movies and songs portray this idea and they aren't wrong. Psychologists believe that it is indeed what happens.

When you fall in love, a part of yourself, and a very important one at that, becomes defined only in relation to the other. Different aspects of our personality are engaged and evoked and amplified by different relationships. For example, you may be an obedient and humble person with your boss, a caring person with your parent, a flirtatious person with your lover and so on.

In an intimate and romantic relationship, we express parts of ourselves that we don't with anyone else; we are appreciated for qualities that perhaps few others would see or recognize.

You and your beloved inhabited your own private world, with shared experiences, ideas, jokes and references that only the two of you would understand, an intimacy further fuelled by attraction and sexual energy, fusing mind, body and soul.

When your relationship ends, it is this part of your self that dies, or at least it feels like that. The aspect of your self that was expressed in that relationship now has no space to express itself, and nobody to validate it. This is a void, and if you were in an intense and intimate relationship, the void is as painful as any grievous physical wound.

Romantic relationships are strongly influenced by the nature of your relationship with your mother. The strength of the bond between mother and child is described in an influential theory called 'attachment theory', first proposed by the psychologist John Bowlby and elaborated by Mary Ainsworth.

According to Bowlby and Ainsworth, infants develop varying degrees of attachment and trust in their caregivers. The most important part of this theory is that the infant needs to develop a good relationship with at least one caregiver, so that he/she can effectively learn how to manage his/her feelings in intimate relationships, later in life. The nature of our early attachment determines the kind of relationships we will have as adults.

Bowlby and Ainsworth described four attachment styles, one secure and three insecure. The insecure attachment styles are anxious-preoccupied, dismissive-avoidant and fearful-avoidant.

In anxious-preoccupied attachment, people want very high degrees of intimacy, need a lot of approval and become overly dependent on their partners. They can feel very angry or hurt at even the slightest hint of rejection from their partner. When their partner is not close to them they feel extremely worried and they often become possessive and worried that their partner will leave them.

In the dismissive-avoidant style, people tend to stay away from intimacy so that they can prevent themselves from being hurt, rejecting the other before they are themselves rejected.

In the fearful-avoidant style, people have mixed feelings about relationships. They feel that they may not be good enough for a relationship, yet at the same time they need a relationship. This conflict makes them avoid people out of fear while craving affection and approval.

People with a secure attachment style find it easier to deal with the uncertainty that comes with intimacy – they are more secure and less dependent on their partners, without being distant. As children, they had a warm and nurturing relationship with their mother, where they were taught how to manage difficult emotions and feelings; a consistent and patient mother helped them feel that they were worthy and lovable human beings. As adults, those with this style usually prefer and choose others with secure attachment styles and have a warmer and more positive relationship with their partners.

Those with insecure attachment styles suffer more intensely (compared with those with secure attachment styles) during heartbreak, and are more likely to be vulnerable to getting into an unhealthy 'rebound' relationship. As you heal from heartbreak, and before you embark on another relationship, consider your attachment style. If it needs to be healed take this opportunity to do so. Practise the exercises in this book, paying particular attention to self-esteem (next section).

Self-esteem

You are a good and valuable person.
You are beautiful and lovable.
You are perfect in your imperfections.

If you are going through heartbreak, you may not believe these statements.

Rejection and unrequited love and pain have made you feel you are not worthy, not lovable, that there is something deficient about you. Negative thoughts like 'I am not good enough', 'nobody loves me' or 'nobody will love me like he/she did' are painfully common.

Why do you feel bad about yourself after a break-up? Why does heartbreak leave you feeling that there is something wrong with you?

To understand this, you have to understand how you derive your self-worth in the first place. You feel badly about yourself now because your loved one's judgement of you has become more believable to you than your own opinion of yourself.

These bad feelings are much worse if your self-esteem was low even before your break-up. When we don't feel good about ourselves, we become even more addicted to love, or a semblance of love, to make us feel valued.

Of course, low self-esteem also causes people to stay on in bad and abusive relationships, since they don't believe that they deserve any better.

Improving your self-esteem is the most powerful way in which you can heal your heartbreak.

The better you feel about yourself, the less the pain of heartbreak. To help your self-esteem after heartbreak, do the following:

- Make a list of the aspects of yourself that you could express in your relationship.
- List out what she/he did or said that made you feel good about yourself.
- List out your personal qualities that you felt good about in your relationship.
- Next, make a list of your strengths that were not expressed or were curtailed in the relationship.
- Give yourself validation. Reading your list of strengths, remind yourself of your many qualities.

- List out the negative comments that your ex has made about you, and rank them in the order of how much you believe the statements.
- Against each statement, think about evidence to the contrary, and write down evidence that proves the invalidity of that statement.
- If there are any genuine negatives, and you would like to improve that area of your life, then make a note.
- Write down your three most positive attributes.

You may also find it difficult to move on from heartbreak because you are dependent on the other person's approval and acceptance. 'I hate him,' she said to me at a therapy session, 'but I still want him to say I love you.' 'Do you miss her?' I asked another client. He thought for a moment and replied, 'I don't miss her, but I miss having someone who thought I was great.' Yet another client spoke of the immense pain that she was experiencing because she felt inferior and rejected. 'When he left me, I felt like my world was over, and then when he started dating another woman, I would often look at their pictures on Facebook and wonder what was wrong with me. Why was I not good enough? I've started to feel bad about how I look, about my personality and even though rationally nothing is wrong with me and I know that sometimes two people cannot get along even though both people are good, I cannot help feeling that there must be something wrong with me because he left me.' Another client said, 'I often wonder what the value of that relationship was. Now I wonder whether it was all a joke.'

Retrieving Your Self

Ideas are powerful and perhaps the most powerful idea of all is that which you have of yourself. *Who do you think you are?*

Psychologists use the term 'self-concept' to

describe what you feel and think about yourself on a conscious and unconscious level. This self-concept determines your choices, your attitude, your expectations, your relationships and ultimately almost everything around you. Your self-concept is pervasive and subtle – it is the filter through which you interpret the world and everything that happens to you.

If your self-concept is 'I am a good, secure, lovable, strong person', you are able to handle the reversals and disappointments of life. But if your self-concept is 'I am an unworthy, weak and bad person, who is not lovable' you can imagine how unhappy and insecure you would feel.

Heartbreak causes suffering because it affects your self-concept. When your heart is broken, you suffer an emotional blow, an attack on your self-concept. Love and the loss of love change your idea of who you are. The closer you were to your loved one, the more dependent you were on the other for your happiness and meaning, the more you will be hurt during heartbreak.

When you are in love and receiving positive signals from your loved one, you may become dependent on those signals to feel good about yourself. Perhaps no other sentence or sentiment is as misunderstood in romance as 'You complete me'. The other person did not complete you. And feeling that they completed you is a misconception that only worsens the pain of heartbreak.

Take the case of Seema, for instance. She is defined by her boyfriend – she thinks of herself only as his girlfriend, she loves his exuberance and, since she is an introvert, she lives vicariously through her boyfriend. She needs him to make most decisions in life and loves dancing with him and going to the movies with him.

She messages him all the time and has to talk to him before she sleeps at night. Physically, the thought of them together fills her with ecstasy and during sex it feels as if she has become completely one with him. This powerful experience is no doubt difficult to let go of, since every part of your being is fused with the other.

The good news is that when it ends you have not actually lost anything. What you think you have lost is still within you. In order to heal from heartbreak, you have to retrieve these aspects of yourself and heal your self-concept. To heal and retrieve the lost aspects of your self, begin by evaluating your current self-concept.

Strongly Disagree	**1**
Disagree	**2**
Neutral	**3**
Agree	**4**
Strongly Agree	**5**

1. My beliefs about myself often conflict with one another.
2. On one day I might have one opinion of myself and on another day I might have a different opinion.
3. I spend a lot of time wondering about what kind of person I really am.

4 Sometimes I feel that I am not really the

person that I appear to be.

5. When I think about the kind of person I was before the relationship, I'm not sure what I was really like.
6. I seldom experience conflict between the different aspects of my personality.
7. Sometimes I think I know other people better than I know myself.
8. My beliefs about myself seem to change very frequently.
9. If I were asked to describe my personality, my description might end up being different from one day to another.
10. Even if I wanted to, I don't think I could tell someone what I'm really like.
11. In general, I have a clear sense of who I am and what I am.
12. It is often hard for me to make up my mind about things because I don't really know what I want.

How to Score

1: Add scores for statements 1, 2, 3, 4, 5, 7, 8, 9, 10 and 12
2: Add scores for statements 6 and 11

1 minus 2 equals the degree of self-concept confusion. The higher the score, the more your self-concept has been hurt by heartbreak.

(This has been adapted from the Self-Concept Clarity Scale in 'Self-concept Clarity: Measurement, Personality Correlates, and Cultural Boundaries' by J.D. Campbell, et al. published in the *Journal of Personality and Social Psychology* 70(1) pages 141–56.)

Loneliness

Heartbreak brings you face to face with loneliness. The end of a relationship leaves a vacuum in your life. You feel alone. Nobody understands you like your ex did, and you feel like nobody ever will.

You will find that most people don't understand your pain, that you cannot share the depth of your hurt with anyone. Indeed, the one person you want to turn to is often the person who broke your heart and now you cannot even turn to him or her. And so the pain of heartbreak pulls you deeper and deeper into loneliness.

Your heart is your bridge with the world, your connection with other people. But when you are hurt, this bridge is destroyed. So you feel estranged from the world, as if there is a veil between you and others. You look out and you see others enjoying themselves, laughing and in love, but behind this thick curtain of heartbreak, you feel disconnected and perhaps even cynical and angry. You might think:

'How silly of them to enjoy love and life. What a waste of time.'

or

'I just don't understand what there is to be happy about.'

or

'They are idiots and fools and they do not know what life's really about.'

What you are really saying to yourself is you feel apart from others. This is loneliness. As human beings, we are the only animal species in the world that has some awareness of its place in the universe. The world is vast and endless, we are born on this planet and we know we are going to die, and being alone evokes terror and isolation in all of us.

Love and attachment are so vital to humans that without these we will die, just as if we have been deprived of food and water. In the early 1940s, the Austrian psychoanalyst René Spitz did a fascinating study on this subject. Spitz was intrigued by an interesting paradox – why were infants in orphanages dying even though they were being given food and shelter? Doctors were puzzled too – infants in well-equipped hospitals actually did worse than infants in less-equipped hospitals. What was happening?

Spitz studied two groups of children from the

time they were born until they were a few years old. The first group was raised in an orphanage where they had little or no contact with caregivers or other human beings. The second group was raised in a nursery in a prison where their mothers were serving a sentence and, in this case, the mothers interacted with their babies every day.

After a year, the difference in the two groups was striking. Infants raised without any human contact were slower to walk, and when they grew older were less confident, angrier and unhappier than the group that had contact with the mother. It wasn't just their minds – their bodies were ravaged by loneliness too. Babies without contact with caregivers suffered from infections and had a higher mortality rate than those with caregivers.

In another experiment the American psychologist Harry Harlow deprived baby monkeys of all contact with other monkeys, without any caregivers or social attachments. By the end of a year, these monkeys were completely dysfunctional. When brought into contact with other monkeys, these monkeys would rock back and forth, refuse to interact with them and shut themselves away in a corner.

So love and attachment are central to us and loneliness causes real suffering. ***Heartbreak provokes a deep sense of isolation, and your suffering during this time can be understood as a response to feeling alone.*** It's completely understandable that for many people the solution to loneliness is to jump into another relationship or to drink too much or to lose themselves in other substances or to simply retreat from the world.

I can't help you get over the pain of the moment but the following points may help you to think about the pain you are feeling and detach yourself a little from it. To break free from the bonds of loneliness, you must reach within and take the first few steps.

- First, remember that you are lonely in a specific way but not alone. Your loneliness is a result of withdrawal from the relationship. Just as a drug addict will crave the drug when he is going through withdrawal, you are craving love and connection. Human beings often believe their emotions, even when the facts are contrary to the feelings. Psychologists call this 'emotional reasoning' or the tendency to believe the emotion. When you feel lonely, you believe you really are lonely, and if you believe you are lonely, you will avoid people and this becomes a self-fulfilling prophecy. So don't believe your emotion of loneliness. Know that there are many people you can and will connect with. You are not alone.

- Stay busy but do not use work as a means to dull your pain. Many workaholics are born in the throes of heartbreak. Or you may find yourself stuck to the old social routine, meeting acquaintances with whom you cannot really share your feelings. Social etiquette dictates that we pretend everything is okay: we feel we have to laugh and enjoy ourselves or behave in a professional and unemotional manner. Interacting in these arenas does not ease loneliness, and only serves to make us withdraw into ourselves even more. Instead, make time for new experiences – go out, travel, join a class, learn a language, meet new people.

- Use this time as an opportunity to reconnect with people who are important to you – friends and family who you may not have had enough time for when you were in a relationship. These experiences will teach your heart that while you may have lost one person, you still have others. Try not to compare those relationships with the one you have just lost.
- Express your pain. Private, unexpressed pain often becomes worse. Identify who you can speak with openly and honestly, someone you can trust and with whom you feel comfortable. If you don't have a close friend or you feel that your emotions

will overwhelm them, seek professional help. Speak with a counsellor who listens to you without judging you. As you speak about your pain, you slowly start building that bridge back into your heart. In talking you connect with others, you connect with yourself.

Mirroring: Seeing Ourselves in Others

Many people find it difficult to let go when a relationship ends because they have a mistaken idea about its meaning and importance. If you're having a hard time dealing with heartbreak and you're having a hard time moving on, it's probably because you gave away some essential parts of yourself to the other person. We often get information about ourselves from the way people close to us treat us. When a person is extremely close to us, much of our self-image is derived from our interactions with that person. This is how human beings are able to live in society and are socialized because we get information from others and we respond to that.

Unknown to you, when you got into the relationship, you may well have derived a great deal of positive affirmation from the interactions with the other person. In fact, most of what passes for love and affection psychologists would call positive strokes or affirmations. There is nothing wrong with these affirmations and positive strokes. Indeed, a lot of healing and happiness occurs as a result.

However, once the relationship ends and these positive affirmations stop, those who do not feel positively about themselves are left with a great deal of pain and misery and will often seek affirmation from the other person as a matter of life and death. Without affirmation, they cannot feel positive about themselves.

If you are suffering from heartbreak and you keep thinking about the other person, how much that person meant to you and loved you, then it is time for you to start taking a clear look at yourself and to ultimately reach a level of self-acceptance. That is the challenge and that is the answer to your problems.

This is a difficult exercise because heartbreak makes it harder for us to accept ourselves. We feel there is something fundamentally wrong with us, that we are flawed, and only the other person, our beloved, can embrace us, ease our pain.

The truth is that you will never find complete acceptance and love from another person – you have no choice but to find it within yourself first, before you seek it from another. If you don't feel acceptance and love for yourself, you will become addicted and dependent on the approval of others and this will make you vulnerable to heartbreak again.

The good news is that no matter how bad you currently feel, ***deep within you is the abiding knowledge that you are a good person, a complete person, one deserving of happiness and love. All you need to do is quiet your mind and notice.***

To prepare for this exercise, find a place where you will not be disturbed.

Sit quietly and contemplate who you are and what kind of person you are.

As you relax, in your mind's eye, see yourself as if from the outside.

When you observe yourself, what do you see? How do you feel about this person?

If you don't feel good about yourself, don't believe those feelings. Rejection and heartbreak can make you feel bad, and render you incapable of seeing your true worth. Allow yourself to experience these feelings, even if they are negative. As you notice without resistance, these feelings will wash over you.

Now gently turn your attention to times in your life when you felt good about yourself – think of the times you felt good about yourself without anyone else having to tell you that you were good. List out the times that you acted with honesty, integrity, purpose, meaning, clarity, happiness, joy, assertiveness and confidence. Even if there is only one incident you can remember and even if it was a long time ago, that's fine. Write it down.

As you begin to get in touch with the vast potential of your real self, you will be able to let go of the need for another person, whoever that might be, to tell you how great you are.

3

The Five Steps to Healing

Walk Away

Begin the process of healing by walking away. It is extremely important to completely end a relationship to get over heartbreak. Heartbreak implies that you still have romantic desire for your ex. And the pain of unrequited love is like raw salt on the wounds of heartbreak. So don't do this to yourself. Let go. As long as you continue to persist in any relationship with your ex, you will get stuck in a cycle of hope, desire and disappointment and find it difficult to get over heartbreak.

But why can't I be friends? So many of my

patients ask me this. Yes, you can be friends, but only if you genuinely have no romantic interest left. I can tell you as a psychiatrist who understands not just the conscious mind but also the subconscious mind that even if you fool yourself into saying 'I am okay being friends' it is likely that your subconscious is still desiring, pining away for the other.

Don't be cruel to yourself. Break free. If you are not getting what you want in terms of a relationship, then do not settle for second best. Swallow the bitter pill in order to get better. Deal with your pain. Understand your own value and walk away.

By this I mean you must **cease all contact for at least three months, following which you could in some cases re-establish a friendship.** During those months, resist the urge to contact or follow him on Facebook or Twitter or social media. Research reveals that staying friends on Facebook is detrimental to the process of recovering from heartbreak.

In fact, Facebook recently unveiled a new feature where they now give you the option of ignoring and blocking your ex so that you will not be tormented by posts and photos that make it harder for you to let go.

Remember that letting go of a relationship is almost like letting go of a bad habit. One that you have become accustomed to. One that offers solace for a while but only to hurt you more. Therefore, to extend the analogy, ***you must be like the alcoholic who always understands that alcohol is dangerous for him/her.*** Your desire for the other, in the context of heartbreak, is like an addictive drug, and you have to fight the craving just as an alcoholic resists the craving of alcohol, until the craving and the pain leave you.

Accept the Inevitable

Ask yourself the following questions:

1. Have I had to work hard to keep the

relationship alive?

2. Has the other person said that the relationship is over in different ways?
3. Do I experience a roller coaster of emotions – hope, disappointment, frustration, waiting – all the time?
4. Do I try to read into her/his words to see if she/he really loves me?

If you said yes to these questions, then this relationship is over. Understand that by staying on, you are chaining yourself to a corpse. Accept that it is over. Let go and you can claim your freedom. When love ends, your heart will fight reality. Move on, your friends may tell you. But your heart will urge you to 'never give up'. This cannot be the end, you will feel. I cannot give him or her up.

And so even though your loved one tells you that it is over you will continue to wait for their call or stalk them on Facebook or ask your friends about them, unable to accept that it is over. It's not easy to accept that the person who loved you does not want to be with you any more.

I bet you even hate reading the preceding sentence. It makes you angry. You may be angry with her or him or perhaps even with me, the messenger. And even though right now you don't feel your life is worth caring about, believe me, it is.

Imagine this.

You are in love again. But this time you are in love with a person even more suited to you than your ex. Heartbreak is the magical rear-view mirror that makes you feel that the relationship that has just ended was wonderful.

I am sure that's not true. If you find yourself saying, 'She/he was so wonderful and we were like soulmates,' stop and remember that if she/he was so perfect for you, you would still be together.

Try to remember now (and write it down in detail) all the frustrations and anguish of being with your ex.

Research has shown that when we remind ourselves of the negatives of a relationship, we are more able to let go.

So remember now and write down in vivid detail the insecurity, the frustration and anything negative that you felt during the relationship.

After this exercise, you will know that what you have lost is not just love, but also frustration and insecurity.

You will know that what you lost was not perfection; who you lost was not your soulmate.

And know this: You will meet someone whom you love even more than you loved your ex, because this time your relationship will be more mature, secure and passionate. The pain you are suffering right now is to help open your heart to a deeper, more secure love.

Better relationships await. You will be happy, relaxed and loved. You will love her (or him) too with joy, passion and openness, like you have never experienced before. So much love that you will realize that you yourself are the source of perfect love, a warm, continuous supply of love that opens your heart and heals your soul.

When you believe and know and have faith

that the future is full of love and acceptance, then you can relinquish the right now. Don't fight it.

I can hear you crying out, 'But I cannot accept it! I won't accept it! Don't you know, you fool doctor, that true love conquers all? My love will persuade her. I will get her back.'

It's not true love that screams and shouts in this way, it is fear. You are so scared of the emptiness and pain that you feel when you consider the end of the relationship that you fight for it, like a drowning creature fighting for oxygen.

You are obsessing. Maybe you think of her with longing and desire, or maybe with hatred and anger, or maybe it's a confusing mix of both. The emotions course through you and your mind cannot move on.

Some people – and please, let it not be you – may frequently check the ex's Facebook account, wait for her call, maybe even follow her and refuse to hear that it is the end of the relationship. But true love doesn't obsess. True, mature love is not forced.

If it requires a lot of work and pleading and bargaining to make someone love you, then you are wasting your time, hitting your head against a wall and hurting yourself even more. The time has come to accept. When you accept reality, you can then begin to heal from heartbreak.

Surrender to a Higher Power

Alcoholics Anonymous is a group that helps people get over alcohol addiction, and some of their guiding principles may also be applied to heartbreak. The most effective of the AA strategies, when it comes to heartbreak, is to have faith in a higher power, to know that something greater than yourself will restore you to peace and happiness.

It's very hard for us to have faith in ourselves. To have faith that things will turn out all right. To know that, one day, even this difficult and painful time will recede. When we face a life situation that we don't have solutions for, we can start feeling helpless and alone. We feel this way because, consciously and logically, we do not feel strong and complete.

But the truth that you must remember, even in moments of pain and despair, is that you have a vast untapped potential and a deep wisdom that is guiding your conscious life. This internal compass and wisdom will lead you out of pain and into fulfilment, if you allow it to. Surrendering to a higher power is a way of tapping into the vast reservoirs of subconscious wisdom and strength.

The times we feel weak and have lost faith in ourselves is when we most need faith. Ironically, ***faith in something larger than ourselves helps us unlock our own inner healing powers.*** And it doesn't matter if you are an atheist or a believer – even the existence of God is not required for you to experience the benefits of surrender and faith.

To know that you will be okay and that you will find happiness again is such a powerful belief that you will at once and immediately feel a sense of relief.

Live in the Moment

'The secret of health for both body and mind is not to mourn for the past, not worry about the future, but to live the present moment wisely and earnestly.' —The Buddha

I can hear you say, 'How can I find peace in the present, when the present is full of pain?' Yes, it isn't easy to live in the present moment, when you are hurting. But consider your pain and the thoughts associated with your pain and ***you will find that your pain is not from the present, but from memories of the past and from worries about the future.***

If you forget about the past and let go of the worries of your future you will immediately begin to feel peace. This is easier said than done, of course, but I urge you to try because as you increase your depth of awareness of the present moment you will start feeling more and more peaceful.

You can begin staying in the present moment and letting go of the past and the future by first focusing on your breath. Make sure that you breathe easily and steadily throughout the day. When we are tense, and stressed, we hold our breath. Our breathing becomes shallow and this pattern of breathing sends a signal to the brain that we are under stress. The stress then further tightens the breathing and so on, in a vicious cycle.

Even though you may not be able to still the thoughts in your mind and your worries, you can break through the cycle of stress and find peace by first stilling your body. When you still and relax your body and relax your breathing, your mind will get the message that you are feeling safe and secure.

Slowly you will begin to notice an increasing awareness of the present moment. It will help you let go of the past, celebrate the future and enjoy the present moment.

When an important relationship ends, we often remember the good and discount the bad times. To get over heartbreak, you must truly understand the relationship. You must see the relationship for what it truly was. The pain of heartbreak is amplified because you are probably overvaluing the relationship.

Heartbreak can make you start glorifying the relationship. What was in fact a painful and frustrating experience might seem like an amazing experience, an opportunity of a lifetime that you have lost. Take a deep breath and begin the process of seeing the relationship more clearly.

To get a more rational understanding of your relationship write down all the things that you did not like about the relationship. Make the list as long and detailed as possible. If nothing comes to mind, break it down into the following categories:

- How he/she behaved with me – Did the other person treat you well, or was he/she disrespectful and uncaring?
- How he/she behaved with others – Was he/she disrespectful or mean to others?
- Personal habits – What habits of the other irritated you, even though you put up with them because you were in love?

- How you felt in the relationship. ***I'm shocked by how many times people say they would love to be with the other person, and yet they describe a relationship where they were constantly feeling upset, sad, angry, frustrated or scared or insecure.***
- Write down all the negative feelings that the relationship aroused in you.
- Write down what you felt when you became aware that the relationship was in jeopardy.

Many people seem to compartmentalize the relationship into the good old days and the afterwards, that is, what happens after the relationship starts going downhill. It is as if the bad part of the relationship is relegated to another compartment and people say, 'Well we would have been happy if only he hadn't had an affair' or 'I would have been happy if only she was nicer to me', 'We were happy until this began' and so on.

This kind of thinking is incorrect. When you compartmentalize and start separating the good from the bad, you are idealizing what you have lost, rather than seeing it for what it truly was. When you think you have lost a great relationship, your pain and sense of loss is amplified. But if you know that what you have lost was never meant to be permanent, you will soon heal.

Our minds also tend to extrapolate from the present into the future. If your relationship was short-lived, it might well have been passionate, fun, exciting and amazing, and with the end of the relationship, you may believe that you have lost a lifetime of such amazing love. But the truth is that if the relationship had continued, it would probably have degenerated, become something quite different.

How do I know this? Because your relationship has ended. And that means that there was already something fundamentally wrong with it. You just found out sooner rather than later.

So if you find yourself thinking about loss, pause and ask yourself, 'What have I really lost? Why did I get into the relationship? Which needs of mine did the relationship fulfil?' Was it loneliness? A need for validation? A need for companionship? Sex? I understand that love cannot be broken down into components, and you may recoil at trying to dissect your relationship in this manner.

Due to idealization, you may feel that your relationship, your love, is beyond such analysis. But the reality is that when you understand why you got into the relationship, you will be able to get out of the relationship.

Geeta, a twenty-something whose fiancé abruptly broke up with her, was distraught when she came to me. I asked her to reflect on how and why she had got into the relationship.

'We met through a common friend. I was actually not interested in him at first, but he kept pursuing me until I agreed to go out for coffee with him. One thing led to another and before I knew it, we were boyfriend and girlfriend.' As she spoke, she became aware of the lack of any real passion in their relationship, and the lack of any intellectual or emotional connection. She also described her own feelings of misgivings about the relationship.

'Did you love him?'

Tears streamed down her face as she thought about it. 'I don't think I loved him, I just got used to him.'

'What are you feeling?'

'Sad,' she said. And then added, 'But relieved.' She was quiet, sad but relaxed, as she mourned a love that she had never felt.

Consider all the lost opportunities while you were in the relationship. Being in a relationship always means lost opportunity. But if the relationship is worth it, then that is a reasonable and healthy trade-off.

However, bad relationships will often inhibit your personal growth. For example, the relationship may have prevented you from pursuing certain interests and hobbies because either your partner didn't allow you to or there wasn't enough time. It perhaps also prevented you from pursuing other deeper friendships. In certain cases, your relationship can take the place of several other relationships and you may lose contact with your friends and even family. Of course this compounds the pain and loneliness experienced during heartbreak but it's also a reminder that you can and you will rebuild close ties with other people.

List out all the opportunities that you turned down or lost because of the relationship. Next, list out opportunities that will be available to you after you heal and move on.

The aim of this exercise is not to create regret – far from it. It is to understand that the relationship was not a great thing to begin with. It ended because it was meant to. And what you will gain is far more valuable than what you have lost.

Learn to Forgive

'The weak can never forgive. Forgiveness is the attribute of the strong.' —Mahatma Gandhi

'Forgiveness is a funny thing. It warms the heart and cools the sting.' —William Arthur Ward

If you are feeling any resentment or anger

towards your ex, then your heart needs the healing warmth of forgiveness.

You may already know what research has proved: anger and resentment can kill you. And that forgiving can heal your body, mind and spirit. One study conducted by Dr Tom Farrow at the University of Sheffield, England, found that forgiving leads to increased activity in the frontal lobe of the brain, the part that is responsible for problem-solving, complex thought and reasoning.

Other studies have shown that forgiveness is associated with a lower heart rate, lower blood pressure and reduced stress. It is also associated with fewer medical conditions and faster recovery from illness.

'I can never forgive him for what he has put me through. Every time I think of him cheating on me, I want to tear him apart, that's how angry I am. How can I forgive him?'

'She broke up with me, and then spread vicious rumours about me. I can never forget how badly she treated me.'

Forgiveness is difficult when you are angry. But that is, of course, when you need it the most.

Anger has trapped you. Forgiveness will set you free.

In order to forgive, do the following:

- Choose to forgive. Remember that forgiveness is an act of great strength. Begin by making a conscious choice to forgive.
- Understand that forgiveness is an act of kindness to yourself too. As long as you hold on to resentment, you continue to be a victim, trapped by the past. When you forgive, you free yourself.
- Forgive yourself first. Before you attempt to forgive the other person, forgive yourself for any real or imagined failings. Many people suffering from heartbreak blame themselves for the situation.

  Ask yourself: Am I blaming myself for the current situation? Am I criticizing myself in my mind, being unkind or harsh with myself?

Would I treat a best friend the way I am treating myself?

If you notice any anger towards yourself, let it go. Be gentler, kinder with yourself.

Treat yourself with the compassion you deserve.

- Forgive your ex. Break free from the past. Remind yourself that your ex is a human being, imperfect and suffering in his own way. Connect with kindness and compassion towards him/her, allowing your heart to heal.

4

Feeling Love Again

The end of your relationship, even if the end was bad, does not mean that your love was meaningless. Your love has meaning even if your beloved was not worthy of your love. To understand this is to begin to set your deepest self towards the path of healing.

Look Within

When you say 'There is no love', then you are indeed unable to see the love within you.

Love begets love and cynicism breeds isolation. To break free from this spiral of negativity, you have to love again. You are waiting for a reason to love. Why should I love again, you ask (consciously or subconsciously).

But you have it all wrong. The problem is that you have always wanted a reason for love. A focus for your love, an external source of love. But love is within you and has always been within you.

Of course, we live in a time where the greatest truths have become clichés and when I say look for love within yourself some of you may dismiss the idea as a New Age cliché that means nothing. Keep an open mind and ask yourself this question: When you fall in love, where is the emotion and feeling coming from? From you, surely.

Yes, you feel that your love is for another, and therefore somehow this emotion belongs to the other. It is true that the other person evoked this feeling within you. But he or she was just the catalyst.

Once the spark of love was ignited, by the presence of the other, you begin to feel that you will feel this only when you're with the other person. What you need is another catalyst, another spark, to ignite the love that is within you and this time you will not make the mistake of believing that the love you feel is from the other person. You will know that love is a gift from the universe to each one of us, and ultimately, at our very core, each one of us is love.

But because we don't know this, we seek perfect love and acceptance everywhere, and each time we fail to get it, we believe that we must look again. Heartbreak is an opportunity for you to stop looking for love and to begin the process of loving yourself again.

To feel and connect with your own core of love, work through the exercises for healing the body, then work through painful emotions such as fear, loneliness and shame. You are then ready to connect with love.

Going Deeper

There was a time when you felt good about yourself. You felt accepted for who you were. You did not think of yourself in terms of good and bad – in fact, you didn't think of yourself at all. Your every need was taken care of, and you felt warm and secure.

We have all experienced pure bliss in our mother's womb. You don't consciously remember the experience, but somewhere within you is the emotional memory of being bathed in warm fluid, your every need taken care, of being accepted and of feeling utterly at peace with yourself. Before you were born (and for a while after), you had no idea of yourself as an individual. You and the universe were one, united in bliss.

Vedanta tells us that you are the universe – pure, timeless, eternal and complete – and that you can connect with your true nature through meditation and contemplation. On the other hand, you are also an individual. A person with a name, an appearance, a personality, and with a role to play in society.

Out beyond ideas of wrongdoing and rightdoing,
there is a field. I'll meet you there.
When the soul lies down in that grass,
the world is too full to talk about.
Ideas, language, even the phrase 'each other'
doesn't make any sense.

—Rumi

When 'you' are hurt, Vedanta tells us, it is only the idea of you, the individual self, that is hurt by heartbreak.

Your individual self believes that you need the other for happiness. It is scared of being alone. Your mind is misled by desire and fear, and tricks you into feeling that you are incomplete without her/him.

But, our ancient texts remind us, you can connect with your real self – not who you think you are, not the name you attach to yourself, not your job, or your looks or your body.

Your true self is beyond desire, and fear, and attachment.

Your true self then cannot be hurt.

Your true self is the eternal, timeless, cosmic self, one that exists beyond judgement, beyond right and wrong, good and bad. It is always blissful.

Your true self is love, peace and happiness.

Western psychologists approached this differently. They studied the individual and explored questions about what makes us unique.

The East explored the cosmic timeless self, and the West explored the mortal individual self.

In order to truly transform from the experience of heartbreak, connect with both – the individual that you are and the eternal bliss that you are, always were and always will be.

Your Unique Individual Nature

What makes you different from others? What are your strengths and talents? If you cannot think of any, then ask your close friends or loved ones. Who were you before the heartbreak? Contemplate your own journey from birth until the start of your relationship. What are your unique qualities? Write down all qualities that you can think of and specific instances where you displayed these qualities. Who do you want to be? Write down a plan for who you can be in three years and your goals in the following domains:

Health: Of mind and body

Career goals

Self-improvement: Hobbies, skills, knowledge

Experiences: What experiences you would like to have in the next three years.

Your Eternal and Blissful Self

You may mistakenly believe that your thoughts are true, that your mind is who you are. Eastern philosophy and meditation practices remind us of a deeper truth: your mind is an instrument, one that helps you or hurts you.

The pain of heartbreak is because your mind has become your master, rather than your servant.

Meditation will help you in a number of ways.

You will feel relaxed in mind and body. You will then connect with the deep quiet and peace, and bliss that exists beyond thought. In this manner, as you become aware of the timeless and enter the undisturbed nature of your true cosmic self, you will heal powerfully from heartbreak.

Let Go of Hope

In Greek mythology, Pandora opens a box full of the world's evils and everything escapes except for hope. Many people are puzzled by the presence of 'hope' amidst other evils.

Hope is the feeling of wishing for a positive and desired outcome and expecting that it will happen. However, hope always has a dark side.

- The desired outcome is usually perceived as vital to life, and the subtext of hope is 'if I don't get what I hope for, my life will not be as good'.
- The desired outcome is usually specific and narrow. Hope says, 'I hope that I will get

that job.' Or in the context of heartbreak, 'I hope she will come back to me' as opposed to a general and higher-order desire, for example, 'I want and know that I will find fulfilment in my career' or 'I know that some day I will feel love again.'

- Passivity and a sense of helplessness also accompany hope. 'I don't think I can do anything about it, but I hope it will happen.'

Hope, in other words, is the emotion that makes you wake up every day, desiring an outcome, not knowing if it will happen, feeling bad about it, but continuing on, only half alive, holding on, until you get what you want. Hope may masquerade as being a good and helpful emotion, but is in fact a deeply draining emotion. It pretends to sustain us, while depleting the joy of the present. Hope makes you anticipate life, and prevents you from savouring life around you.

'Yes, I know I am alone now, and I am hurting, but when she is back with me I will be fine. It looks bad, but I hope and pray every day that we get back together.'

'I lose hope sometimes, but then I get a message from him and it gives me hope again. I have another boyfriend, who is a nice guy and he wants commitment from me, but I don't want it, since in my heart of hearts I hope that my ex will be back with me.'

When I look into the eyes of a person sustained by this kind of hope, I see sadness and, worse, I see a person disconnected from the beauty of life around him, unable to accept the end of the relationship. Many people cling to the hope of even a slim chance of getting back together with their ex.

And even though they seem to move on, they do not commit to another relationship. They hold back, saving themselves for a love that may not return. I am not suggesting that hopelessness is the answer. As psychiatrists, we know that hopelessness is a devastating emotion, one that pushes a person to suicide. 'There is no point, everything is hopeless. I might as well die now.' To heal from heartbreak, let go of hope and embrace optimism instead.

Embrace Optimism

Optimism is the feeling that good things will happen, but it does not carry with it the same passivity that hope does. There's the old joke about two boys, one a perennial optimist, the other a perennial pessimist. The parents were worried about the extreme personalities and took the boys to see a psychiatrist.

First the psychiatrist took the pessimist to a room full of brand-new toys. But instead of delight and happiness, the boy burst into tears. 'Don't you want to play with any of the toys?' the psychiatrist asked. 'Yes,' the little boy cried, 'but if I did, the batteries will run out and I will only end up breaking them!'

Next the psychiatrist took the optimist to a room piled to the ceiling with horse dung. But instead of reacting with disgust, the optimist shouted out in happiness and began happily picking up scoop after scoop of dung. 'What are you doing?' the psychiatrist asked, puzzled by this response. 'With all this dung,' the little boy replied, smiling, 'there must be a pony in here somewhere!'

Pessimism and optimism are lifelong attitudes, and it's not easy to change your perspective. And yet, heartbreak is your invitation and opportunity to cultivate a more optimistic attitude.

A pessimist is often more hurt by life events because of his interpretation of the event. When a negative event occurs, a pessimist is more likely to interpret it as being:

- Personal – The negative event is my fault. (If I wasn't such a fool, this would not have happened.)
- Pervasive – The negative event affects everything in my life. (I am not just an idiot at work, I am also an idiot in my personal life.)
- Permanent – Life is always going to be this

way. (I will always make stupid mistakes like this.)

Worse, when a positive event occurs, the pessimist will say that it is:

- External: The good event has nothing to do with me, but is because of some external event. (Yes, our team won the prize, but it was mainly because of the other guy's efforts. I got lucky.)
- Situational: The good event is only limited to this situation and the rest of life continues to be negative. (I guess I am good at research, but I am so bad at everything else.)
- Transient: Good times never last. (Today's a good day, but I know what's going to happen, tomorrow or the day after, or very soon, I will get bad news. That's how it always is.)

So in this way, the pessimist is unable to feel happy irrespective of whether a negative or a positive event occurs in his life.

An optimist reverses the process. When a good event happens the optimist interprets it as being:

- Personal – The positive event is because of my talent. (I am great at singing, and I've worked hard at it.)
- Pervasive – The positive event extends to other areas of my life. (My hard work paid off here and I know it will pay off in other areas of my life.)
- Permanent – Life is always going to be this way. (Sure, there are some bad times, but for the most part, life turns out fine.)

And when a bad event happens, the optimist says that the bad times are:

- External: The bad event has nothing to do with me, but happened due to external factors. (I made some mistakes, but the tech team messed up too. They didn't communicate clearly and that was part of the problem. Let me figure out how to deal with this so it doesn't happen in the future.)

- Situational: The bad event is only limited to this situation and the rest of life continues to be positive. (This project is going badly, the customer is difficult but I have a great time with my colleagues and friends. So it's not too bad.)
- Transient: Bad times never last. (It's a bad day, but I know it's going to get better. I don't even remember what I was worrying about last year.)

Pessimists are more likely to suffer from the pain of heartbreak. But heartbreak is an opportunity to transform your attitude from pessimism to optimism. Notice how you interpret events. Notice what you say to yourself. If you find that you are interpreting events in a pessimistic manner, stop and take another look.

When you are faced with a disappointment

in life, write down an optimistic interpretation of the event, as described above. When you have a positive experience, ensure that you reward yourself emotionally, just as an optimist would (as described above).

Write down why heartbreak will not last, and how you will use this experience to discover your own strength and positivity. In this manner, cultivate optimism and the pain of heartbreak will dissolve in positive energy.

Conclusion

In a scene from the television show *Louie*, a stand-up comedian asks a cranky old doctor, 'What should I do about my heartbreak?'

The doctor's reply is unexpected. 'You think spending time with her, kissing her, having fun with her, you think that's what it was all about? That was love? You are wrong. THIS is love. Missing her, because she's gone. Wanting to die...

You're so lucky. You're like a walking poem. This is the good part.'

Louie cannot understand. 'I thought this was the bad part,' he says.

'No!' the doctor says. 'The bad part is when you forget her, when you don't care about her, when you don't care about anything. The bad part is coming, so enjoy the heartbreak while you can, for God's sake.'

Yes, you have suffered. Perhaps more intensely than you have ever before.

But the experience of heartbreak is perhaps the closest you have come to what it means to be human. The human experience is about pain and joy, experiences that remind us that we are alive. That we feel. Far too many people in this world are numb as they go about the daily routine of living. They have never loved as intensely, and never felt the deep pain of lost love.

But life had different plans for you.

Because of heartbreak, you came face to face

with deep questions about yourself and about life. You had the courage to explore these questions as you embarked on a difficult inner journey. You stared your psychological demons in the eye, wrestled with your fears and insecurity, until you found your way to the deep and abiding love that is and always will be within you.

Some day when you look back, you will realize that both the joy and the pain shaped you, and made you stronger. The pain is a testament to your capacity to love. And heartbreak is a reminder that you will love again.

Appendix

How to Heal Your Body

To heal your body, it is important first to nourish your body adequately. Yes, your mind tells you there is no point in eating, you have no hunger or desire for food, everything seems colourless because your loved one has left you – and yet food is a vital form of energy. If you can reconnect with food, that will be one step closer to reconnecting with love.

All emotions are felt in the body. For example, when you are angry, your thoughts are angry, your breath is rapid and shallow, your abdomen clenches, your heart rate increases and your muscles contract. The sum total of your thoughts, your hormonal changes and your bodily response is the experience of anger.

To let go of anger, you have to not only let go of your thoughts but also change the bodily response. Many people mistakenly believe that when the mind stops feeling the emotion, the body will follow. However, the relationship between mind and body is bilateral – the body is not a mute and silent slave to the mind, it also exerts its own influence on the mind.

If a person is angry for a long time, the body will hold on to the tension, and even if the situation has passed and the person's mind is at ease, the body will continue to send signals of threat and anger to the mind.

To let go of these emotions, you must first be aware of that pain.

Through the body awareness exercise, you will now be aware of the emotions in your body.

Exercise, Yoga and Pranayama

The best exercise programme for heartbreak is a combination of aerobics, breath exercises and yoga.

Any cardiovascular exercise like brisk walking, swimming, cycling or playing a sport is a great general tonic for the mind. Exercise boosts your mood and energy levels.

I usually advise against running initially since it is a high-impact exercise and is not for everyone. Ensure that you are fit before you start running. The best initial form of exercise is brisk walking. Start with walking at least 20 minutes a day three to four days a week.

In addition, practise the following pranayama and asanas to help release anger, fear and sadness. Begin with warm-up stretches and five rounds of surya namaskar.

Next practise the following asanas:

Bhujangasana
Shalabhasana

Dhanurasana
Veerasana
Savasana

Follow with 15 minutes of pranayama, specifically anulom vilom and ujjayi.

Massage and Acupressure

The skin is the largest sensory organ of the body, and is the organ through which our body feels nurtured and loved. Through therapeutic touch and massage, powerful feelings of nurturing and support, which were lost during heartbreak, can be communicated to your body and mind. Unfortunately, professional, well-trained massage therapists are expensive and hard to find but you can learn self-massage and acupressure techniques that will help you heal.

Organic sesame oil has a long history of use in Ayurvedic practice and when used as a massage oil regularly it decreases anxiety and stress.

Lightly massage the oil all over your body, using long strokes of light pressure. Next massage the following areas: base of thumb, knees, ankles, navel, chest, neck muscles, temples.

Apply pressure with your thumbs and fingers to these areas, all the while breathing evenly.

Press any areas of discomfort with your thumb until you feel a mild tenderness.

Focus your awareness on the area of contact between thumb and body and breathe as if the air is entering your body from that pressure point.

Hold for three breath cycles and release.

Eating Right during Heartbreak

Often, people reach for junk food to mitigate the pain of heartbreak. The craving for junk food is very similar to the need for drugs and alcohol. While it may offer you temporary respite from the pain, it will only wreak more havoc in the longer term. Every time you eat high-sugar, high-fat, high-sodium-content food such as French fries, pizza, burgers, chocolate cake, cookies, ice cream, chocolates, they cause a spike in your blood sugar and your brain might mistakenly interpret this as happiness. This surge of temporary pleasure is fleeting and will leave you drained, tired and sadder and far more lost and empty. No amount of bad food can fill the emptiness that you're feeling. Your emptiness comes from emotions and not from a physical need.

The food that you eat during heartbreak must be soothing, nurturing and comforting and yet safe and healthy. Often, this could be food you enjoyed as a child. Try to eat home-cooked, healthy food. If not, try to cook healthy, nourishing food for yourself. The act of cooking and taking care of your needs can also begin the process of nurturing yourself. Not everybody has the energy to start cooking for themselves right away. If that is the case with you, just source healthy food. The meal should be largely vegetarian with plenty of fruits and vegetables. The carbohydrates can be either wheat or rice. If you are from a predominantly rice-eating region, continue to eat rice since our genetics depends on years of environmental conditioning. If you are from a wheat-eating region, stick to wheat. Ensure that the amount of meat and animal protein is less than 10 per cent of your caloric intake and try to avoid meat for at least a few weeks. If you cannot, then reduce it to a bare minimum. Avoid the following: fried food, fatty food, any kind of processed food, including packaged noodles. Avoid store-bought fast food. Read the label and avoid any food with a high sodium content.

Ensure you are eating a variety of fruits and vegetables. Also take omega-3 fatty acid supplements from fish oil or flaxseed oil. These nourish the central nervous system and will aid your recovery. While it is common wisdom that you should eat frequent small meals, this is often not possible when you're suffering from the pain of heartbreak. However, it is important that you do not starve yourself during this time because starvation can increase the amount of hormones in your blood, leading to greater distress. You are already feeling a lot of stress from the heartbreak and it is essential that you do not tax your body. If you find that it is very difficult for you to eat, try to eat small amounts of your favourite fresh fruit. If you find it unpalatable you can sweeten it with honey or brown sugar. Also ensure that you get adequate exercise which stimulates your appetite.

Do not eat highly spiced food especially after 8 p.m. since it will interfere with your sleep. However, it is not vital that you avoid spices all together.

Breath Awareness and Relaxation

When we were in our mother's womb, our connection to everything that kept us alive was the umbilical cord. We received nurturing through our navel and our body remembers this even when we have consciously forgotten the experience. When we are hurting from heartbreak, ***a common area of tension and pain is the abdomen, especially around***

the navel. It is as if the navel constricts itself, saying, I am not getting any nurturing, no point opening up to the world.

Similar constrictions are felt in the region around the heart, which is literally the physical abode of love. The chest also tightens and is often painful to touch. The throat constricts, almost as if there is so much pain that it cannot be expressed.

According to ancient Indian texts, we are composed of energy called prana that flows through channels in the body called 'nadis' and meets at nodal points called 'chakras'. When prana flows freely, we are connected with the blissful energy of the universe. When there are blocks in prana, we feel depressed, sad and tired, and disconnected from bliss.

These ancient concepts are not accepted by modern western science, but after more than fifteen years as a doctor and psychiatrist, I know the limitations of modern science and psychiatry.

Susan went through heartbreak when her fiancé broke up with her abruptly and without explanation. A year later, she could talk about the relationship without feeling pain, and she stopped crying when describing the suddenness of the break-up. However, whenever she got close to someone, she felt uncomfortable and scared.

She could not understand this fear. 'I know that the break-up is in the past and that I can love again. And yet, something is holding me back. I like this guy and he likes me but whenever he comes close to me, I cannot help feeling scared,' she said.

I taught Susan how to pay attention to the signals from her body and to her breath patterns. When she came back to the next session, she had some interesting observations. 'When I felt we were becoming closer, I felt afraid. Then I noticed that my chest area, over my heart was feeling tight. I also felt a knot in my stomach and my throat.'

This is actually quite common. Modern medical science would explain this away as nothing but muscular tension occurring due to stress. It's interesting though to note that the areas of constriction are centred at the energy nodes or 'chakras'.

When people undergo heartbreak, their pain usually aligns with the seven major chakras located in our body:

1. Lower abdomen
2. Navel area
3. Solar plexus
4. Chest over the heart
5. Throat
6. Forehead
7. Top of the head

Susan meditated to become aware of the feelings of threat and loss that were still lurking and blocking her energy. As she released this pain, the knots eased and in a few weeks she felt much better.

Frequently Asked Questions

Do men and women handle heartbreak differently?

Women are often emotionally stronger than men. In general, they have a stronger emotional brain and they navigate the world of feelings better than men. Compared to men, women also usually form deeper emotional ties with friends. They talk more about their feelings, and are more comfortable revealing their vulnerabilities.

Men are often taught to be 'strong' and not to cry or express pain. Men may have close friends but don't usually speak to their buddies about their feelings.

When hurt, women are more likely to seek support and to express their feelings. Men feel angry, irritated and hostile and will often retreat into their shell. Women tend to surround themselves with healing relationships; men often isolate themselves and alienate others with their anger and pain.

The new Indian man invests more in feeling and is the more emotionally dependent one in the relationship. Men put all their (emotional) eggs into one basket and therefore, when the relationship ends, they are devastated.

Researchers studied the emotional responses to break-up in more than 5000 men and women from ninety-six countries. They found that while women suffer more pain from heartbreak, it takes men much longer to recover.

Even more startling was the finding that men never fully get over their break-ups. They often just move on to the next relationship without exploring or becoming aware of what went wrong in the previous relationship (http://psycnet.apa.

org/psycarticles/2015-30907-001). So men suffer more and learn less from heartbreak than women.

How can I get closure when the other person is not telling me why he/she broke up?

A big misconception is that we can get closure from the relationship by speaking with the other person. When you are suffering, it is natural to ask the question: Why did he break up with me? And you wait for the answer, unable to move on, as if the explanation is the key to the lock that imprisons you.

Remember this: Even your partner does not know why he/she broke up with you.

You will not find a satisfactory explanation because a break-up is the result of multiple complex subconscious forces. Reasons cited may vary from incompatibility to commitment phobia but these explanations are not the whole truth.

He may have actually broken up with you because he had an overprotective mother and, subconsciously, he feels smothered by intimacy and closeness. She may tell you that she does not feel any passion any more, but the real reason may lie in her chaotic childhood of emotional neglect. Your care and concern make her unsociably unnerved, and unsettled, since it contradicts what she learned about intimacy as a child. She may be seeking chaos rather than stability and so she breaks up with you.

If you are hoping that the other person will provide closure, you are allowing the other to continue to hurt you.

So how do you find closure?

First, by appreciating the complexity of the reasons for the break-up and giving up the questions: Whose fault was it? Why did we break up?

Second, by knowing that you can get closure by reflecting on it yourself. That the truth of why you broke up has to be your truth.

Instead of thinking about it in terms of fault and blame or in black and white, start by writing the narrative of your relationship from the first meeting to any big events, good or bad, during your time together, and then the events leading up to the break-up.

This may take a few days, don't hurry. Then read this story as if you are reading the story of someone else's life. Ask yourself: Why did this couple break up? Why did the relationship end? Write down the factors responsible for the break-up. Which of your needs were not fulfilled? Some key needs for a good relationship are trust, respect, affection, sex and attraction, intellectual compatibility, companionship and the feeling of being understood. Were other factors incompatible? For example, personality, interests, cultural values, mood issues. Was there abuse or infidelity? Were there extended family issues? Write down the negative emotions you felt during the relationship.

Once you complete the above, you will see the complexity and the many shades of your relationship; you will see that there is no one reason that you broke up. And that it was ultimately beyond your control. There is nothing more to analyse or dissect or understand about the relationship. You have found closure.

Is heartbreak only felt by the person who was left behind? What about the person who made the decision to break up?

It's a common misconception that heartbreak is only felt by the person whose love is unrequited, the person who was left behind, the person whose partner broke up with him.

It is true that when the other breaks up with you, you are often shocked, bewildered and hurt, and it may even seem that you are the person who is suffering more.

However, the person who does the breaking up suffers as well.

First, any and all the symptoms of heartbreak described in this book apply to both parties – whether you broke up or the other person did, both of you will feel the pain and suffering associated with heartbreak.

People who have left this relationship for another may have just postponed their suffering.

The person who breaks up carries the additional burden of responsibility. They made the decision and now they must live with the consequences of their actions.

Regret is also a painful emotion. Many people who break up find themselves thinking and rethinking their decision, second-guessing themselves, wondering if they have made the right decision.

If they move on to another relationship, and that doesn't work, they may look back at the break-up and regret letting go of what they once had.

I have seen some people devastated years later by the break-up that they had initiated.

How do I know when I am over the person? How do I know when I have healed from heartbreak?

You will know that you have healed when you feel happy and complete, even without that person; and this feeling of happiness and fulfilment is from within you, without the addition of any other toxic or harmful behaviour, substance or relationship.

You will not be angry or cynical. You will feel love – love for friends, for family, for the blessings in your life.

You will feel relaxed in mind and body. You will make healthy lifestyle choices. You will be open to new experiences in life. You will have the capacity to trust again and to share your feelings in an intimate relationship.

Why is a rebound relationship unhealthy?

A rebound relationship is one that you get into while still suffering from heartbreak. The new relationship eases the pain and suffering of heartbreak and the danger is that you mistake the easing of pain for genuine love.

Do not get into another relationship while you are still suffering from pain, especially severe heartbreak. Once you are a bit better, you can begin to meet people, but when you do so, be aware of your own vulnerability and need. Engage your rational mind as much as your emotional side. Evaluate the other person, and your compatibility, before getting too close.

At the same time, research tells us that a good relationship heals and helps one get over heartbreak. The key here is to ensure that your pain, or need for love, does not propel you into another even more complicated or difficult relationship.

Although every situation is different, I would recommend a period of three to six months at least before you think of dating again or getting into a new relationship.

The more the heartbreak and the more severe the suffering, the more time you need to heal.

The best kind of relationships to have during the time of heartbreak are non-romantic, non-sexual relationships – friends and family.

You may also want to consider getting a pet. If you cannot have pets, you can even get a small houseplant – watering the plant every day and tending to it will also ease the pain of heartbreak.

Is heartbreak more common nowadays? Why?

In the old days, relationships survived for a long time, often for a lifetime. People didn't date and the only person they were intimate with was usually their spouse.

Roles were clearly defined in marriages. Choices to stray outside the marriage, especially for women, were limited. Women were not independent and often had to stay on even in bad marriages because of economic reasons.

Nobody expected their partner to fulfil all their needs – emotional, intellectual, sexual. Practical considerations were most important – the ability to coexist and function together in clearly defined roles.

Today's India is very different. For the first time, millions of young men and women are dating, trying to find their own life partner.

There are several shades of intimacy and different kinds of relationships, other than marriage – from dating to friends with benefits to open relationships to occasional hook-ups, from Tinder to Hinge to Facebook and WhatsApp, today's world offers men and women much more choice.

But choice also amplifies dissatisfaction – because of technology and a changing society, there is a greater tendency to compare one's partner with another person, and often small differences become intolerable.

People are also more stressed than ever before. Long commutes with high expectations at work mean that men and women get little time to spend with each other.

Without time, relationships wither and die. Stress and sleep deprivation compound the issue. Couples often become impatient and intolerant of each other, and the relationship falls apart.

More than men perhaps, women have changed in what they desire from a relationship.

Roles were more clearly defined in marriages, and even in the brief courtship and dating of past generations, the woman generally acquiesced to the man, allowing him to play the more dominant role in the relationship.

But equations have now changed in the new India.

The new Indian woman is finally free to make choices, to earn her own living and to be defined in her own right and yet she is reeling from the memory of her gender's subjugation by men.

She knows that her mother's generation and the generations before derived their self-worth and identity from the family. Many Indian women find this idea frightening and abhorrent. The most important value for many of them is freedom. Intimacy poses a threat to this need for autonomy for a couple of reasons.

In any intimate relationship, you have to balance your needs with the needs of the other, and the need for compromise can appear scary and claustrophobic, especially when you desire a lot of freedom.

Many Indian men, threatened by the freedom and autonomy of their partner, unfortunately exert control and dominance – because of insecurity the man may try to dictate what she can wear, how she speaks, how she behaves, and so on.

Of course, this attempt at control only increases the woman's desire for freedom and autonomy and often the relationship ends.

Compared with the previous generations, today's Indian man feels much more insecure in relationships and this is a trend that I believe will grow.

Indian women will also first have to explore their own need for autonomy and freedom and have to learn to balance the many roles they play.

I loved him/her more than he/she loved me and I feel terrible about it. Was my love a waste? Am I a weak person?

There are people one might term 'shallow', who may not feel very deeply even though they have been with someone for so many years. In these cases, the person who is less intimate and whose feelings are less deep will often move on, without any emotional repercussions. The person who felt more deeply and is consequently more hurt will compound his or her hurt by feeling even more trivialized and marginalized. It is as if we believe that if a person is not interested in us then they must be superior to us. This is a very strange and fairly universal misconception. Perhaps it comes from the human tendency to believe that that which is scarce is valuable, like diamonds or gold. For many people, love that is easy to get and easy to sustain is of no value and has no meaning.

It is therefore quite possible that a person who is more committed ends up feeling needy, unworthy and even more fragile and insecure compared to the person who loves less. Let your pain be a reminder of your own sincere love, but do not overestimate the value of your beloved.

Many relationships are based on the fact that people presume and believe that the relationship will carry on for a long time, perhaps through a lifetime. In fact, great romances believe that love will transcend a lifetime and carry on through many lifetimes with the souls being intertwined. When this kind of great expectation and love ends, a person starts to feel bereft. They feel as if they've been robbed not only of the future, but also the past. What does it all mean? Was that love meaningless? Maybe he/she never really loved me. These are the questions and doubts that come to the mind.

It's very important to understand that, no matter how close you are in any relationship, your experience of the relationship is ultimately yours alone. And the other person's experience of the relationship is ultimately theirs alone.

A relationship is like a shared dish. Each person has his share from the same bowl and enjoys it, but their perceptions and their experience and their reactions might be very different. A relationship is a joint endeavour, a construct co-created by two individuals. However, the same reality is experienced very differently. Therefore, you get to define what the relationship meant for you and what role the relationship played in your life. And so does the other person.

If you loved and loved sincerely then that has great meaning and value, even if the other person was not worthy of your love. Some day, your love will find a more suitable recipient.

Acknowledgements

Writing is not a solitary project. This book would not have been written without the many people who encouraged and supported this project and I want to extend my deepest appreciation and gratitude to them.

To my parents, fortunate enough to love without heartbreak, for giving me unconditional love, encouragement and support, thank you for everything.

To my sister, Deepa Bhat, an epitome of patience and empathy, who is always there for me, even when I don't return her calls.

To my children, Rishi and Kirtana, who bring

love and laughter to my life, thank you for being you.

To Somil Mittal, restaurateur par excellence and all-round nice guy, with an intuitive understanding of human nature, thank you for your unwavering support of my writing.

To my friends with whom I have had long conversations about love and heartbreak: Sundeep Rao, Sanjay Manaktala, Ahmed Shareeif, Uma, Sunayna, Radynee, Bops KJ, Ekta Patil, Anirban Blah, Nina Nair and Archana Mittal.

To Anna Chandy, brilliant therapist, and dear friend, whose intuition and compassion has helped so many – thank you for our conversations about human nature, for your insights, and support.

A mega thank you and gratitude to Deepika Padukone – you are a star, but more important, you are a star human being. Thank you for your inspirational strength and honesty, for speaking up, for acting on your convictions and for caring, and for your initiative the Live Love Laugh Foundation, which will transform the way India feels about mental health, and ultimately save thousands of lives.

To Priya Ramani, editor, thank you for your support, encouragement and insight.

And finally a huge thank you to Chiki Sarkar, publisher extraordinaire, and founder of the amazing publishing house Juggernaut for being the only person who could have made sense of the chaos of my initial draft. You made this book happen, thank you!

A Note on the Author

Dr Shyam K. Bhat MD is a psychiatrist, integrative medicine specialist, and writer. He is the founder of Seraniti.com and a trustee at the Live Love Laugh Foundation, founded by Deepika Padukone. This is his first book.

AN EXTENSIVE LIBRARY

Including fresh, new, original Juggernaut books from the likes of Sunny Leone, Praveen Swami, Husain Haqqani, Umera Ahmed, Rujuta Diwekar and lots more. Plus, books from partner publishers and loads of free classics. Whichever genre you like, there's a book waiting for you.

juggernaut.in

DON'T JUST READ; INTERACT

We're changing the reading experience from passive to active.

Ask authors questions

Get all your answers from the horse's mouth. Juggernaut authors actually reply to every question they can.

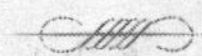

Rate and review

Let everyone know of your favourite reads or critique the finer points of a book – you will be heard in a community of like-minded readers.

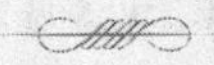

Gift books to friends

For a book-lover, there's no nicer gift than a book personally picked. You can even do it anonymously if you like.

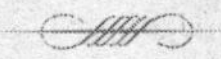

Enjoy new book formats

Discover serials released in parts over time, picture books including comics, and story-bundles at discounted rates. And coming soon, audiobooks.

LOWEST PRICES & ONE-TAP BUYING

Books start at ₹10 with regular discounts and free previews.

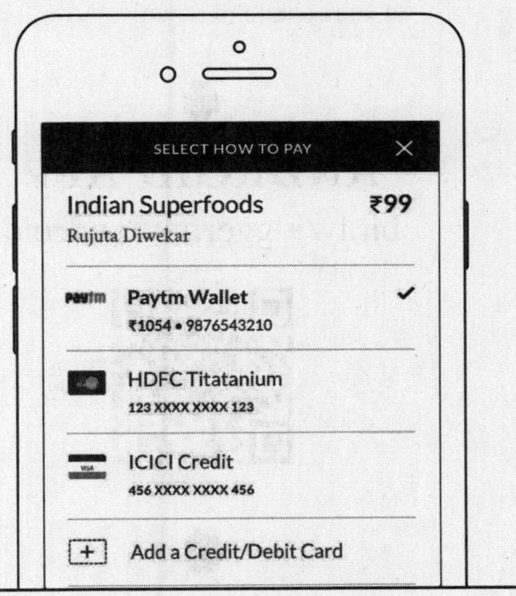

Paytm Wallet, Cards & Apple Payments

On Android, just add a Paytm Wallet once and buy any book with one tap. On iOS, pay with one tap with your iTunes-linked debit/credit card.

Click the QR Code with a QR scanner app
or type the link into the Internet browser
on your phone to download the app.

ANDROID APP

bit.ly/juggernautandroid

iOS APP

bit.ly/juggernautios

For our complete catalogue, visit www.juggernaut.in
To submit your book, send a synopsis and two
sample chapters to books@juggernaut.in
For all other queries, write to contact@juggernaut.in